Lettice

A & M

forever...

First published in hardback in Great Britain by HarperCollins Children's Books in 2005
First published in paperback in 2005

1 3 5 7 9 10 8 6 4 2
ISBN: 0-00-771990-6

HarperCollins Children's Books is a division of HarperCollins Publishers Ltd.

Text and illustrations copyright © Mandy Stanley 2005

Visit our website at: www.harpercollinschildrensbooks.co.uk

Printed and bound in Hong Kong by Printing Express Ltd.

Lettice

The Bridesmaid

Mandy Stanley

HarperCollins *Children's Books*

Lettice Rabbit and her family lived high up on top of the hill. Nibble, nibble, hop, hop, every day was the same but one day...

Lettice popped her head out of the burrow
and saw a letter fluttering on a bush.
'It's for ME!' she squeaked!

Lettice

Paws shaking, Lettice opened the letter.
It said:

Dear Lettice

I am getting married very soon.
Will you be my bridesmaid?
Come and see me today and I'll tell you all about it.

Love
Your dancing teacher
Giselle xxx

Lettice wiggled with excitement.
A bridesmaid! What was that?

She scampered over the hill to her dancing teacher's house.

'Come in, Lettice,' laughed Giselle. 'I've got something special to show you!'

Giselle's room was full of
snow-white ribbons and sparkling jewels.
Hanging up was a beautiful white dress.
'Oooh!' whispered Lettice.

Suddenly, the dress twitched. Lettice stared as two hands appeared.

A boy scrambled out from under the dress. 'This is Harry. He's going to be my ring bearer at the wedding,' said Giselle.

'Harry,' said Giselle, 'on the day, my wedding ring will be placed on this cushion, which I'd like you to carry.'

Then she gave Lettice a basket and explained, 'You will scatter flowers in front of me as I arrive to get married.'

Next, Lettice was measured
for her bridesmaid's dress.
'It'll be made especially
for you,' said Giselle.

Lettice raced home with an invitation
for the whole family. She couldn't
wait to tell everyone all about
the wedding.

On the morning of the wedding, Lettice got up very early.

Her mother was getting the little ones ready.

Soon it was time to leave.

Lettice hopped across the meadow,
gathering the prettiest flowers
for her basket.

Giselle looked beautiful in her wedding dress.

'Harry,' said Giselle.
'Here is the ring.
Don't lose it!'

'Come with me, Lettice,'
she smiled. 'It's time for
you to put on your
bridesmaid's dress.'

Gently, Lettice unwrapped her clothes. 'Just for me?' she whispered.

First, she wiggled into the petticoat...

then she tied the ribbons on her slippers...

...and placed some flowers on her ears.

Finally, Lettice put on her new dress.

'Now I really am a bridesmaid!' she sighed, swishing the skirt.

At last it was time for the wedding to begin.
Lettice took a deep breath and scattered
her flowers. They flew up in a coloured cloud.
As Giselle walked by, Lettice waited for Harry.

But Harry looked very worried.
'The ring!' he gasped.
'It's GONE!'
Lettice couldn't
believe her ears.

Quickly, they
searched along the
gravel path...

...and in amongst
the flowers.
Harry began
to cry.

Just as he pulled out his handkerchief, Lettice saw something glinting.

'The ring!' she shrieked.
'It must have slipped into your pocket!
Quickly, we must catch up with Giselle!'

George beamed with happiness as he saw his bride arrive with Lettice and Harry.

And when Giselle said, 'I do,' everyone sighed.
It was the most beautiful wedding
they had ever seen.

Later, Giselle had presents for Lettice and Harry.
'I want to thank you both for helping to make this
the happiest day of my life,' she said.

'And I have a present for you,' said Lettice.

She twirled and whirled...

...and spun around in her own special dance, just for Giselle.

The moon was up by the time Lettice and her
family set off home. Lettice was so tired that
her father had to carry her to their burrow.

'It's been a perfect day,' she whispered
sleepily. 'The most perfect day of my life.'

Lettice

Collect Mandy Stanley's adorable books about
Lettice - the little rabbit with big dreams!

0-00-716584-6

0-00-716583-8

0-00-716581-1

0-00-716582-x

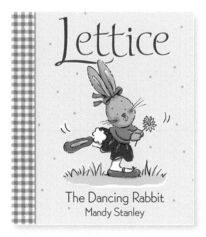

0-00-664777-4

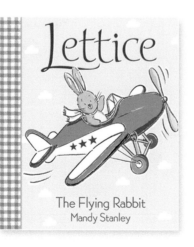

0-00-714197-1

0-00-716585-4